100%
Devotion

100% Devotion

...Where the Devotee Disappears and only God Remains

By **Sirshree** Tejparkhi

Copyright © Tejgyan Global Foundation
All Rights Reserved 2019.

Tejgyan Global Foundation is a charitable organization
with its headquarters in Pune, India.

Published by WOW Publishings Pvt. Ltd., India.

First edition published in June 2019.

ISBN: 978-93-87696-87-7

Copyrights are reserved with Tejgyan Global Foundation and publishing rights are vested exclusively with WOW Publishings Pvt. Ltd. This book is sold subject to the condition that it shall not by way of trade or otherwise, be lent, resold, hired out, or otherwise circulated without the publisher's prior written consent in any form of binding or cover other than that in which it is published and without a similar condition including this condition being imposed on the subsequent purchaser and without limiting the rights under copyright reserved above, no part of this publication may be reproduced, stored in or introduced into a retrieval system, or transmitted, in any form, or by any means, electronic, mechanical, photocopying, recording or otherwise, without the prior written permission of both the copyright owner and the above-mentioned publisher of this book. Any person who does any unauthorized act in relation to this publication may be liable to criminal prosecution and civil claims for damages.

Contents

	Preface	5
1.	Devotion—What and Why?	7
2.	Role and Benefits of Devotion	14
3.	How, When, and Where to Practice Devotion	29
4.	Levels of Devotion	38
5.	Principles of Devotion	53
6.	Receptivity and Miracles in Devotion	61
7.	Deepening the Practice of Devotion	69
8.	100% Devotion	86

Preface

The journey that you have begun to meet God is called devotion. The path of devotion begins with appreciation and praise for the external nature—the abundance and blessings found in this world. When you reach closer to your destination, praises for the nature within you begin to flow from you. Before reaching this state, you may have some questions about devotion.

This book is a selected compilation of questions posed to Sirshree by various seekers. The queries in this book range from the meaning of devotion to the crux of devotion. Every answer is intended to clear your beliefs about devotion and help you cultivate true devotion. Devotion will lead you to God. If you don't believe in God, it will lead you to the ultimate truth—the truth about you and the universe.

The journey towards God or ultimate truth or liberation comprises of two major paths: Knowledge (*gyana*) and Devotion (*bhakti*). Actually, both are essential to reach your destination. Knowledge can help you achieve liberation, and some people feel that knowledge is enough. But there is the possibility of developing ego of knowledge and thereby getting stuck in the cosmic illusion (*maya*) once again. Devotion helps you to remain established in the liberated state. Devotion gives you the power to easily overcome the obstacles to liberation—

the mind, its ego and various tendencies. It helps you to lead a truly successful and peaceful life amidst these chaotic modern times. It adds joy and music to your journey towards divinity and endless bliss.

Using simple stories and analogies, this book tells you everything about devotion; including its various aspects, its principles, its numerous benefits, as well as indications on how to develop devotion and reach its height. It also reveals what is the ultimate purpose of devotion or what is 100% devotion.

With practice, you can progress from the first to the tenth level of devotion, where you realize that God and you are not two different entities—both are one. Such bliss! But then you may choose to separate from God once again. Why? Only because you love the experience of devotion so much! Such is the sweetness of devotion. So, let's begin this fascinating journey.

1

Devotion—What and Why?

Seeker: What is devotion?

Sirshree: Devotion means falling in love with love itself. To understand this, consider this sentence: "God is love; love is God." Why is it said that God is love? When we understand this, only then will we get the insight on how falling in love with love is devotion. Let us consider an example. Supposing a person loves to dress up in various ways and take his own pictures in different places. What would you say about such a person? Probably that he loves himself very much. Likewise, God manifests Itself in infinite forms, in order to express Its love and joy in different ways. *All the beings (living and non-living) of all the universes are various photographs of God Itself!* (1) Then just imagine how much God loves Itself. Even today It is engaged in discarding its older pictures and creating new ones all the time. That's why it has been said that God is love.

So, when you fall in love with God, you fall in love with love itself. This is devotion.

Seeker: You referred to God as "It"?

Sirshree: *Actually God is beyond he, she, or it. It can be said that either all forms are of God, or no form is God. God is the nothingness from which everything arises.* Therefore, whether we say 'He,' 'She,' or 'It,' they all refer to the One essence. So, any one of them can be chosen for ease of communication.

Seeker: Got it. What I don't understand is, why one should practice devotion when there are many other paths that lead to the truth?

Sirshree: There are many paths that lead to the truth, such as *gyana* (wisdom), *dhyana* (meditation), *karma* (action), *japa* (chanting), self-enquiry, devotion, etc. But they can broadly be divided into just two: the path of wisdom and the path of devotion.

The path of devotion is that of surrender to the divine will of God. It is the path of submitting to Consciousness—the Source of everything. *Effort in this path is effortless, as actions happen in joyous surrender to God, or the Self, or Consciousness, or whatever name you want to give it.* The path of wisdom is that of willpower, where seekers of truth apply their intellect to grasp the truth and internalize it.

The path of devotion is akin to a kitten, which leaves its body loose and gives itself up to its mother, who then carries it around with her mouth. The path of wisdom is like that of a baby monkey that needs to clasp its mother's belly while she jumps from one branch to the other. The kitten surrenders. The baby monkey clutches with all its might. All the paths that are known in spirituality finally culminate in this two-fold path—one approach is that of complete surrender, while the other is that of intellectual reasoning and meditation. The seeker of self-realization needs guidance on both these paths.

Seeker: Do both these paths lead to the same result?

Sirshree: Let's understand this with an example. There were two travelers who needed to cross safely through a jungle to return home. One of them was blind, while the other was a cripple. Individually, they could not have made it home. Hence, they made a decision. The cripple climbed on the shoulders of his blind companion and guided him through the jungle. The blind man followed his directions and walked carefully, carrying him through the jungle. Both managed to reach home safely.

So it is on the path of self-realization. The crippled man symbolizes the eye of wisdom, while the blind one represents the legs of devotion. *Without the legs of devotion, the eyes of wisdom cannot walk the path. The legs of devotion cannot see the path without the eyes of wisdom.* Therefore, let devotion acquire the eyes of wisdom and let wisdom in turn receive the legs of devotion. The seeker who pursues the path of wisdom through the practice of meditation and conscious action develops unswerving faith, thereby leading to the surrender of his individual ego to the Self. The one who follows the path of devotion matures in understanding of the truth. *Finally, the one who works on attaining wisdom surrenders, and the one who surrenders attains wisdom. Thus, both the paths merge at its culmination in stabilization in the Self.*

However, you do not have to decide which path is best for you to begin with. Whatever the mind prefers need not be the best path for you. Following the path that the mind feels like is like asking a thief how he would like to be captured. Leave how this happens to divine grace. Ultimately, grace is the only way!

Seeker: Okay, but I thought devotion was something that was practiced by saints in the past. I did not think it was important in these times and for the average person.

Sirshree: *Devotion is not an outdated concept practiced by certain saints of yesteryears. It is important even today and will always remain so, because it helps you to know and experience your truth as well as the truth of this life and this universe.*

It establishes you in the state of supreme love and bliss. It helps you to attain God. And when you attain God, you attain everything; because everything is a creation of God. So, perhaps now you may agree that devotion is important for everyone.

To commence your journey of devotion, spiritual knowledge is required. As soon as the thirst for truth arises, an individual sets out on the quest for knowledge. But knowledge alone won't quench your thirst. *A seeker may pass through various paths for attaining the truth but does not experience inner satisfaction. For that reason, one must turn to devotion.* We must have faith that there are certain laws of the universe that are operating, whether we understand them or not. We must believe that only when we become self-realized we will understand.

The most difficult fact for most people to comprehend is that we are both the Created… (by God)… and the Creator (God). We are one. We are different aspects of the same—whether you call it God, Ishwar, Allah, Lord, Self, Consciousness, Witness, Nature, Creator, Supreme Being, Higher Power, the Source, the truth, or any other name. Devotion will help you realize this truth and live this truth.

When you first heard the word "devotion," what was your thought? You may have shied away from it, thinking it's for devoutly religious people—*not me, not for us ordinary mortals going about our lives!* You may feel it has no relevance in your life. You have heard about it, but it did not occur to you that it's for you, that you greatly benefit from it. The simple fact is that you cannot attain the truth without devotion.

Seeker: Performing rituals and prayers at certain times is devotion, right?

Sirshree: Perhaps you follow a religion, participating in the rituals and repeating the prayers or mantras, and you have faith, but you don't fully understand what you're doing or why. You may think that devotion is lighting a lamp or a candle and bowing before the Lord at a particular time and then you are done! You may feel that devotion has no place the rest of the day because, after all, you have to be practical to live in this world! That is why most people confine devotion to their places of worship or to a certain time. *But you don't live **with** devotion, you live **in** devotion while managing all the practical aspects of life.*

Seeker: Who has the time for such devotion?

Sirshree: Many people love to complain that they don't have time for devotion or other spiritual pursuits (outside the obligatory religious services). But when one comes to know about a celebrity coming to their town, or about a sporting event, they never miss that opportunity. How do they manage to find the time? *When you understand the importance of meeting God, you will find time for it because it is so incredibly joyful that you won't want to waste your time on meaningless pursuits, ever again.*

Shri Ramakrishna has said, give one hand to the Lord as you perform your duties in the world, and once your work is done, give both your hands to God. Suppose someone has a throbbing boil on his back, he will still continue with his day to day activities and also engage in conversations. But a part of his attention will be on that boil at all times. Similarly, you can keep a part of your awareness consistently on God; it is possible.

When your devotion will be coupled with understanding of the truth, it will be divine devotion. When you contemplate and dig deep within due to devotion, it becomes divine devotion. *The irony is, many people don't like the idea of devotion until it awakens in them. But once it is awakened, it becomes everything. You will still go about your daily chores, but with a knowing inside, a joy, an understanding, and an all-pervading peace that knows God. This makes it possible for you to say, "Thy will be done."*

Seeker: I would feel scared to say, "Thy will be done."

Sirshree: If you understand the true meaning of 'Thy Will Be Done,' you will lose all your fears. Perhaps you feel fear or hesitation thinking that you don't know what God's will is and how it will affect you. But ask a true devotee about it. They will tell you that *this proclamation arises not only because you love God, but also because you know that God loves you more than you ever could, and hence there can be nothing better than God's will or God's divine plan for you.* ⑭

Secondly, *when you attain the supreme truth, you realize that God or Self is not someone else or something else, it is who you truly are. How could you want anything but the best and highest for yourself? With this realization, you can easily and fearlessly proclaim: "Thy will be done."* ⑮

These four words can change your life. These words contain the purest expression of surrender to your true self. These words are not only a mantra but a prayer, which can take you closer to your true self if you repeat them with feeling and faith. If you can believe in the prayer of these four words, then it can dissolve every problem of your life. ⑯

2

Role and Benefits of Devotion

Seeker: I have understood that devotion is important, but is it really essential?

Sirshree: Suppose somebody asks you, "Why do you eat food?" You may reply, "I eat food because I feel hungry and I need to satisfy my body's requirement of energy and nutrition." Then if you are asked, "If you don't get energy or nutrition from food, would you still eat it?" To this, you would most probably say, "Yes! I would eat food simply for the enjoyment of it!" You would say this because the experience of eating for satisfaction is complete in itself. In the same way, *devotion is complete in itself. It is complete joy and fulfilment in itself.*

Devotion is in fact a blessing endowed to us. Most people believe that God is pleased if they practice devotion; however, the reality is that we are in devotion because God is pleased. Devotion is not possible if God is not pleased with us. God is bliss and devotion is its expression.

Devotion has a role both before and after attaining the truth. It is the path and the destination, and also beyond the destination, because it pervades the supreme state of nirvana. That's why the glory of devotion is being sung since ages. The most wonderful aspect of devotion is that it is relevant and beneficial through all the stages of spiritual evolution.

Seeker: Who should be in devotion, or in other words, who actually surrenders to God—the body or the mind?

Sirshree: The body cannot act on its own, until the thought of action arises in the mind. If you don't get the thought "wake up" in the morning, your body cannot wake up. The thought always precedes the action. Thus, *the body is utilized to demonstrate and express devotion, but devotion originates in the thought—the mind.*

When we go to a place of worship, our body bows, but has our judgmental mind ever bowed? Have our thoughts ever bowed? Have we ever reached the state beyond thoughts? Probably not. Because the mind is an obstacle in the path of attaining the truth. If there are thoughts of the material world in the mind, then your journey is outwards. But when you receive guidance from a true master, then your journey is inwards and you reach the place of origin of thoughts—your center, your heart, or your *tejasthan* where the Self connects with the body—where there is unbroken bliss and stillness. So, in order to be in devotion, the mind must be in devotion.

Seeker: Can devotion be developed at any age or by any type of seeker? What impact does it have on each of them?

Sirshree: Devotion can be attained at any age and by every seeker.

When a meditator attains devotion, they no longer remain high and dry; they are immersed in the ocean of supreme love.

When a knowledgeable person attains devotion, they lose the ego of their knowledge and become *Bright Ignorant*. (Bright ignorance is a state beyond the duality of knowledge and ignorance).

When a yogi attains devotion, they do not remain stuck in their yogic powers but achieve the power of devotion.

When a worldly individual acquires devotion, they do not remain a slave of this illusory material world but instead become a *Bright Householder*. (Bright householder is a state which is beyond the duality of a worldly person and an ascetic. It's the state in which an individual practices spirituality while carrying out all their worldly duties.)

When a child attains devotion, they do not remain ignorant but become wise like Bhakt Prahlad (a child devotee from Hindu mythology, well-known for his devotion to Lord Vishnu).

When a teenager attains devotion, they give up their wild ways and become like Saint Gyaneshwar (a renowned teenage saint from Maharashtra, India).

When an elder person develops devotion, their fear of death ends because they realize the immortality of life. They therefore bypass death and enter the eternal grand life.

This is what devotion means in different states and at different stages in the journey of life. Devotion makes the complete journey meaningful and beautiful at every place and every stage. It is never too late to start on your path of devotion!

Seeker: What difference does devotion make in our actions, our responses, and our life in general?

Sirshree: When devotion is at the superficial level, it remains at the level of feelings and does not translate into actions. Deep devotion means complete devotion that comes from feeling into action. Thereby every action and every response of the devotee is filled with devotion, which arises from the feeling of love, joy, and stillness. This is in contrast to the individualistic response that emerges from ego, vices, or faulty beliefs. *When you develop devotion, you change and so do your actions. With a new response, you invite newness in every aspect of your life.*

If you want to attract a new life, then check which seeds you are sowing in the present. If you are repeating the same actions which are based on old beliefs passed on from one generation to the next, or actions based on addiction to vices and tendencies, then you will see the repetition of the same past scenes from your life.

If you have given importance to devotion, it will begin to reflect in your feelings, thoughts, words, and actions. Your response to people and situations will be filled with devotion. The mind's habit will urge you to give the old, conditioned response but now you won't be helplessly delivering the old response. *When you start living in devotion, you become free from old habits and tendencies and hence free from destiny, because you give more importance to the will of God.*

Devotion is such a marvelous gift from God which improves and enhances all areas of life. Not only do you achieve spiritual growth but also progress at the mental, social, financial, and physical levels. Devotion also helps you to easily come out of your comfort zone. Usually, when all your routine tasks are over and then if you are told to do something new, the mind immediately resists. With the power of devotion, you would be ready to go the extra mile. Thus, you are able to leave behind your comfort zone and discover your capacity and potential. You develop the ability to achieve any goal you desire. You won't think that if you are unable to do certain activities at present, then you can never do them in the future. On the contrary, you will think, "Though I have been unable to do it at the first try, but I want this thing to happen. Dear God, You can do it through me."

Devotion helps you to get through trials and tribulations of life gracefully. If you are able to give even just your spare time to God and engage in spiritual practices, it ushers a positive change in your life. It would create a new and bright future.

Another aspect is that often people get stuck in the belief of being great or superior to others on the basis of religion, caste, nationality, skin color, etc. This feeling takes one away from devotion. In fact, some people are considered as devout devotees because they religiously follow all the rituals and even teach the scriptures, but if they haven't understood the essence of devotion, then they may have been liberated from all labels except the label of being superior. *Devotion liberates you from all labels of superiority and enables you to see the One in everyone.*

Seeker: What is the impact of devotion on wisdom?

Sirshree: True wisdom is beyond knowledge. True wisdom comes with devotion, with the attitude of surrender to life. It comes with unconditional acceptance to the way life unfolds.

Devotion transforms knowledge into wisdom. *Devotion inspires faith on knowledge and also helps you to experience that knowledge, rather than just knowing it at the intellectual level.* Intellectuals may slip on the path of truth, but devotion comes to their rescue and uplifts them once more. In fact, it's devotion that helps you to persist on any spiritual path, if you have reached a plateau or have diverted or backtracked.

Devotion also saves you from developing the ego of knowledge. Additionally, it helps you to make new and better choices in spite of your patterns. Otherwise, after attaining knowledge, people feel they are wise but still cater to their tendencies and patterns. In that case, they are no different from people who haven't attained knowledge; rather they are more egoistic than the others.

With devotion, the spiritual journey not only becomes easy but also very sweet. If you so desire, you can attain the final truth with knowledge too, but for that you need to have an intense thirst for the truth. With devotion, you can attain the truth with a light and joyous spirit. With knowledge, you need to work with depth and awareness, because there is a risk of getting entangled in knowledge.

An intellectual seeker builds a guitar and a devotee plays it. The intellectual uses his brain and does so many calculations to build a guitar. But it's the devotee who uses it to sing praises of the Lord. The intellectual designs the temple, but the devotee sings and dances in it, as the bliss overflows in him. The intellectual creates colors, but who plays with the colors during Holi? The devotee!

Seeker: What is the relation between devotion and *sattvaguna* (equanimity)?

Sirshree: The basic disposition of every individual body is either *tamoguna* (lethargy), *rajoguna* (hyperactivity), or *sattvaguna* (equanimity). These *gunas* are what drive you and your actions in this world. Each has negative and positive characteristics. You progress from tamas to rajas to sattva. Sattva is a good state for a seeker. There are people who take pride in leading a *sattvic* way of life—a life of piety, equanimity, and balance. They in fact develop the ego of being sattvic. They consider a sattvic way of life as their ultimate goal, but that's not so.

Besides, *sattva* alone feels quite dry and dull later on. If life becomes disciplined and straight, if there is sincerity, maturity, and simplicity, with time the individual is likely to start feeling bored. If one is walking straight since a long time, one will say there's no enjoyment. Hence, very often people reach the state of *sattvaguna* and then slip back.

This is where devotion plays a crucial role. It prevents the individual from slipping back or giving up. The sweetness of devotion makes one continue on the path of truth. Otherwise, they won't be able to muster the strength required to transcend sattva and reach the gunateet state (the free state which is beyond rajoguna, tamoguna, and sattvaguna).

The important point to understand is that all three *gunas* bind your true self to the body and you are unable to attain the free state. Devotion will help you reach that state. When you are attached to the body with devotion, you can fully experience and express the Self through your body. The attachment of devotion with the body is light and loving. This attachment helps in liberation of the Self, or in other words, unification with God.

Seeker: What is the relation of devotion with karma and meditation?

Sirshree: Performing karma in the spirit of wisdom is true devotion. Performing awakened action in the light of recognition of the Self is devotion. *Devotion helps you recognize the God in everyone and everything and thus perform the best karma.*

Devotion reduces your attraction towards the illusory world. As there is the law of attraction, there is the law of repulsion as well. *The law of attraction works for meditation; this means devotion starts attracting you inwards and you start practicing meditation to connect with the God within you.* You can use the law of attraction for prayer too to attain what you want.

On the other hand is the law of repulsion—where your repeated attention to God and devotion actually pushes away or repels the illusion. If you take devotion with you while going into the world of illusion, then all it takes is to hear some word that reminds you of God. Sometimes your attention does go towards the illusion, but your devotion can be at such a high level that your focus automatically shifts from the illusion with complete ease and love. Let this law of repulsion work in your life too.

Seeker: But then how will we succeed in the material world?

Sirshree: Don't be under the impression that if the law of repulsion operates in your life, you won't attain success in the material world or that your attention would be distracted from the factors that are essential for living. The law of repulsion simply raises the level of your devotion. It won't have any negative effect on your success. You can certainly make use of the law of attraction for becoming successful and for progressing in other aspects of your life. But remember that your spiritual progress should not stop by getting entangled in illusion.

Seeker: Isn't power or social status important?

Sirshree: They are important, but the level of your power should never be more than the level of your devotion. Otherwise, people work only for money, status, or power. This does not mean that you should not work to earn money, but watch where your focus is and what your feelings are behind your actions. *If your actions or karma are filled with devotion, selflessness, and the intention of well-being of all, you would automatically get everything you need because you get rewarded by nature in multiples for your selfless (impersonal) work.* Until people experience this, they say this is illogical and impossible. And that is why they do not even begin to lead an impersonal life. Domination is the desire of power; whereas helping you to accomplish your ultimate purpose on Earth is the desire of devotion.

When your mind attains devotion, it begins to develop discipline. Then a time comes when it becomes prepared to surrender and dissolve in devotion. That is when unconditional devotion begins. Initially, people have a lot of expectations and conditions related to devotion. For example, they want to achieve material objects, they want their desires to be fulfilled, and they want all their problems to get solved... if all of this happens, only *then* do they feel they are ready for devotion.

But the reality is that all these things come automatically with unconditional devotion. You easily and spontaneously receive everything in abundance; but remember these are all just a bonus. Devotion is complete and fulfilling in itself and hence let your devotion be unconditional.

Seeker: How does devotion help us in achieving our spiritual goal?

Sirshree: God, Consciousness, or Self wants to express its highest potential through the human body. The main qualities of the Self are love, happiness, stillness, courage, praise, creativity, etc.; and the highest form of expression occurs through the bodies that are ready. Those that are not, are under the influence of wrong tendencies and they express the ego. *The biggest hurdle between the Self and the body is the ego. In spiritual terms, 'ego' means the sense of a separate identity; the sense of apparent separateness from the rest of creation as well as the Creator. Due to presence of this primary ego, man remains deprived of the highest wisdom and expression.*

You can win over the ego with love and not by fighting it. This is possible only if you give the highest priority to devotion.

First of all, you will have to quiet the ego with love. It is not so easy to quiet the ego because it says, "Why am I being told to be quiet? I am important!" If someone loves you unconditionally but you are not aware of it, then you don't give them the right response. But the moment you become aware of it, your response changes. Likewise, *when you realize that it is unconditional love, joy, and the experience of pure consciousness that you are receiving from the Self, your ego begins to surrender.*

Devotion also liberates you from your tendencies, which are a hurdle in attaining the truth. Devotion adds joy to the whole process of spiritual growth. Attaining the truth is not difficult, it is easy. The difficulty that one faces is due to one's tendencies, the habit of forgetting the truth, and the lack of thirst for the truth. That is why every seeker has to work on these three aspects. Everything becomes easy with the surrendering of tendencies, because then your awareness level rises and you start living with awareness all the time.

Spirituality is always available and nobody can stop it. But many people in fact enhance their tendencies in the name of religion. Tendencies are such that even religious people get caught in them. Unfortunately, such so-called religious people use their tendencies for acquiring higher positions or to bring people under their control. In this way, a good thing like religion also starts misleading people. Consequently, the purpose of religion is lost and the supreme truth cannot reach people.

Those religious leaders who are entangled in their habits and tendencies think that if they tell the supreme truth to the masses, they will lose control over them. And so, they don't disclose the truth to the people. When spiritual leaders stopped telling the truth to the people, the effects of this went unnoticed for some period, but when people were deprived of the truth for many many years, then so-called "religion" began controlling the people. Those who hid the truth (real religion) also forgot it with time.

When an individual starts digging and undergoes a spiritual journey in quest of the truth, he or she then attains the truth. Devotion encourages us to keep aside our tendencies and give importance to the truth. Devotion teaches us to stand steadfastly with the truth. It also gives us the strength to continue on the path of truth even in the face of great hardships and hurdles. If you read about the life of great devotees like Sudama, you will realize the extent of hardships he faced. Yet he lived his entire life in accordance with the knowledge and instructions received from his master, only because of devotion.

Seeker: How does devotion help in breaking our tendencies or patterns?

Sirshree: There was a master and he had two disciples. One of them had the duty of serving him water and the other of serving him food. One day, the one who served him water was not available. So, the master asked the other to give him some water. The disciple replied, "That's not my duty. It's not my job to give you water."

This means this individual has caught hold of the form of service. "I have been given this duty. This is what I have to do." A true devotee is ready to do whatever God desires. The attitude of getting stuck in one aspect of service, is like being caught in a pattern. Every human being is stuck in one's patterns. Patterns have become your obstructions. Women have their own patterns, and so do men, and if there is no devotion, they cannot get out of their patterns. Sometimes, in relationships, people get out of their patterns for the sake of love, but when the tide turns, they get back to their old patterns. They get angry with each other and go back to their usual tendencies.

But *when a devotee's love for God is true and deep, they willingly and gladly do whatever is God's will and for that they need to break all their old patterns.* If God is not happy when you feel and act like a limited individual, then due to devotion you will be prepared to transcend it. So, ask yourself, "Which patterns of mine is God not happy about?" If you link your patterns to God's happiness, it will be very easy to get rid of them. The intellectual increases his willpower and uses his own driving force. Whereas, a devotee knows, or wants to know, about the patterns that God wants him to let go. Then if at times you need to serve water, or at other times you have to serve food, you won't have any resistance.

This is the beauty of devotion, that the biggest patterns can be dissolved. And if devotion has awakened within you, take full advantage of this opportunity.

Seeker: At which level or state does one feel that devotion is a boon?

Sirshree: When devotion comes into action, that's the state in which one feels that devotion is a boon. Devotion begins at the level of feelings, then it comes to the level of thoughts, then in speech, and in the end it comes into action. As the influence of devotion increases in our life, it starts expressing through our actions at the same pace, and then we reap the fruits of our devotion. Devotion then starts feeling like the greatest blessing of all.

As such there is no rule for devotion, but one starts with some rules for making it a boon. Later on, everything goes beyond rules. When devotion comes into action, its power destroys your ego and all your tendencies. You are able to let go of all those things that you could not earlier due to greed. No willpower is necessary when devotion comes into action. If all of this is happening in your life with the power of devotion, it means devotion has become a boon for you.

Seeker: Is it true that as soon as devotion awakens within us, everything looks good and right, and all our complaints disappear?

Sirshree: No, it's not true that as soon as devotion begins, everything will appear nice and fine and all your complaints will disappear. It is necessary to ripen in devotion with *sadhana* (spiritual practice). As soon as you develop devotion, you start feeling good. And the more this good feeling increases, the easier it becomes for you to compromise and let go in various situations that appear in your life. When you are feeling bad, you get irritated at even minor things. When you are feeling good, you are able to forgive someone very easily.

The great creations of the world have taken place only through happy creators. In a happy state, creation takes place in lesser time and it is of high quality and high vibration. When a group of people work together on a project, it is natural for conflicts to arise between them, but if everybody's goal is devotion, they would easily unite and move forward. Happy creators very easily forgive each other and join forces for the common goal. Thus, complaints will arise even after you have developed devotion, but you won't dwell on those for a long time. That time period will go on reducing.

With time you will realize that everyone is a part of you. *The God in you is dealing with the God in everyone else. All your transactions are with God alone.* With this realization, you will stop feeling hurt as well as hurting or blaming others. You will feel convinced that everything is happening in your life for the progress of Self, for you to reach the highest level of consciousness. You will lead your life with the conviction that going forward, everything is going to be the best, and thus you will operate with joy.

When you reach the height of devotion, all complaints vanish from your life because the separate individual, the false 'I,' disappears and you become empty like a flute. Then there is nothing left from where complaints would arise. Only four words remain: Thy will be done.

3

How, When, and Where to Practice Devotion

Seeker: How can we develop devotion?

Sirshree: You can listen to discourses that convey the truth, contemplate the truth, read books that contain the truth, and pray for the truth. "Dear God, I wish to attain divine devotion. Let love and devotion arise within me and spread through me. By looking at me, let devotion awaken in the hearts of other people too." You can sing hymns, read stories of devotees, and join a group of devotees. When you are in the company of other devotees, you too are bound to get imbued by their devotion. You too will get immersed in the sweetness and beauty of devotion. Think and speak about devotion as much as you can. After all, it's nature's law that whatever you focus on will grow in your life.

Another way is to be in a constant state of gratitude and appreciation. It's easy to appreciate the miracles and be grateful

(39) for the abundance and blessings in your life, but *an important step in your spiritual journey is the realization that everything, whether you consider it good or bad (duality), is in your life for the purpose of your growth and progress towards stabilization in the Self.*

Devotion is possible for everyone. Nature has created methods to encourage devotion in everyone, such as: beauty (have you ever been moved to tears by something beautiful?), resonance (the feeling of music remaining in your body long after the sound is no longer heard), kindness, compassion, unconditional love of a mother, etc. Thus, even in this material world, one can be in devotion. When you reach such a state that tears start flowing from your eyes as soon as you utter the name of God, it is clear that you are in devotion even while residing in this materialistic world.

Seeker: Why should tears flow in devotion?

Sirshree: When a saint worships God in the form of Mother Goddess, he prays, "O Mother, when will the moment come when I will just utter your name and tears would start flowing from my eyes? Oh, dear mother! When will this happen?" Can you imagine what's in the mind of this devotee? Why do they want to have tears? Who would have such feelings? To understand this, you need to read stories of various saints and sages. Look for the revelations of understanding that they had underlying their prayers.

(40) *Tears of devotion do not trouble the devotees. On the contrary, they give them supreme joy, they cleanse and purify them internally, and flush out their bad tendencies.* This is the understanding

with which the saints offer the prayer. Only those who shed tears of devotion realize its joy.

People who have only the knowledge of truth don't realize this joy because they first understand the truth with their intellect and only later can they correctly pray for attaining the ultimate aim of life. Earlier they use prayer to acquire worldly objects. They do not ask for God Itself. *Many people strongly believe that they receive whatever they ask from God. It does not occur to them to ask for God from God.* As soon as you ask for God from God, you see the opening of the road to the truth. Here you realize the need for both knowledge as well as devotion.

Seeker: What is the role of chanting?

Sirshree: The practice of chanting was created by some enlightened souls with the intention that by doing so, people would begin their journey towards God. This is because they may be unprepared for receiving higher knowledge right in the beginning. Therefore, in ancient times, people were asked to simply chant the name of God. The main purpose behind this was to eventually convert this habit into prayer, which in turn would become powerful with repetition. Consequently, they would get further guidance or message from the universe and proceed accordingly.

People follow the ritual of chanting, but they never think about the underlying purpose. They fail to appreciate or even recognize the many forms of guidance that they receive from the universe as a result of their efforts: a message, a book, an experience, an image, a hunch, or something else, which are often dismissed as unimportant in favor of rituals. Suppose a person is chanting and somebody comes and tells them, "Let's go for this *satsang.*" They say, "Please don't disturb me. Let me continue with the chanting. I don't want to do anything else." Thus, they are unable to catch the message sent by God for their further growth.

That's why the one who practices chanting should be alert and open because a divine message or command in any form can come to them at any time. When they receive it and work in accordance with it, only then will they benefit from the chanting.

Seeker: When should one practice devotion? Is there a specific time for it?

Sirshree: Devotion knows no time. However, when beginning with devotion, it is helpful to establish a routine—a fixed time, fixed place, in a fixed posture, and using a fixed method. When you do this, your mind becomes habituated to it. Then, at the specified time, the mind automatically becomes tuned to that inner work. This helps prevent the mind from resisting the cultivation of devotion, as it may in the beginning. After some practice, the mind will start immersing in devotion on its own.

Mornings and evenings are the transition times between the night and the day. In devotion, you are seeking to bridge the gap between yourself and God, and these junctions or transitions represent the junctions within you. Since ancient times, these periods are used as prayer times in India. If the purpose of engaging the mind in devotion is fulfilled, then the purpose of these junctions is served.

In the beginning, practice devotion during the time period when the mind is ready to support devotion. However, *devotion is often wrongly seen as something to be practiced only at certain times. When the mind is filled with devotion, then no moment passes without it.*

Seeker: Where should one practice devotion?

Sirshree: After Saint Namdev attained the supreme truth, one day God visited him. "Why don't you come to the temple nowadays?" asked Lord Vitthal. Namdev bowed and said, "Dear Lord, if I go to the temple assuming I'll find you there, it means you are not here. That would be like insulting you."

This little story indicates that *God is everywhere. In other words, God can be worshipped anywhere. Devotion can be practiced anywhere.* However, don't assume that there is no point in visiting the places of worship like temples, churches, mosques, etc. Do visit the places of worship—they are peaceful and may inspire greater devotion in you; but don't assume that God resides *only* in those places or that you can meet him *only* over there. God is with everybody and everywhere. God is in everything and everything is in God. Thus, devotion can be expressed anywhere.

Seeker: How can we get rid of obstacles like fear, worry, dilemma, etc. during the early period of devotion?

Sirshree: During the early period of devotion, you will definitely encounter some difficulties because during that time your devotion is not stronger than your tendencies. When your devotion rises even a little above your tendencies, you start overcoming fear, worry, dilemma, etc.

Your tendencies and behavioral patterns increase your problems. That is why you need to dig deeper into those problems and look at them with a new perspective. Thus, you need to support your devotion with knowledge. You need to ask yourself, "Is the problem which is creating a hindrance really that big, or does it only appear to me as so?"

Whenever you face any dilemma, you can pray, "I want the joy of clarity and freedom. May my presence at any place be always filled with love, joy, and stillness. May divine bliss fully manifest in my life." With this prayer, you sow the seed of faith.

Be in the present and enjoy it. Appreciate, learn from, and enjoy every present moment—the good as well as the bad. When you deeply reflect upon every complaint and every story that you have in your mind about others, you will grasp the reality, and the feeling of happiness will go on rising within you. Then even when you remember the past events of your life, the memories will only give you joy.

During the early part of devotion, all these aspects will teach you to love everything that is coming in your life. You learn to see the blessings in your adversities.

Every year, school students have to appear for their exams. Many kids feel stressed, but if they have the right understanding, they can enjoy that stress and use it to their advantage. Stress helps to strengthen and stretch their wings, so that they can take off in life. Until the stress appeared, their wings were stuck inside and power was needed to open those wings. The stress of the challenge provides that power.

The right prayer soon ends the stress as well as the entanglement in the problem. You begin to see the complete solution. If you overcome one problem with understanding, then you will be saved from all further problems.

Seeker: On the path of devotion, how do we know whether we are progressing or regressing?

Sirshree: Imagine that you are going towards a garden that you cannot see from where you are now. The garden is alive with the beauty and bounty of nature. Magnificent trees and fragrant flowers await your appreciation and enjoyment. You are on a path leading to the garden, and you are being guided towards it. In this case, you are guided by your sense of smell. If your nostrils experience a foul smell, then you would know you are not on the path to the garden; and if you are receiving a pleasant fragrance, then you are on the right path.

On the path of devotion too, you receive such indications that let you know whether you are progressing on the correct path. *If your attention goes on the good qualities or virtues of people, it means you are on track. If your attention always goes on others' flaws, it means you are not on the right path.*

Seeker: What takes us away from devotion and how to prevent it?

Sirshree: When you believe the events taking place in this illusory world to be true, you fall away from devotion. People are highly influenced by what they see, and they believe whatever they see. Today, the need for *satsang* is felt by people because of excessive negative impact of events occurring in their lives, such as failure, relationship issues, financial issues, career problems, etc.

(45) *In satsang, people start seeing their actual purpose (which is invisible) on this Earth.* The highest creation that God is creating for you is invisible. Creation is the quality of God. God wants to pass on all His qualities to every one of you, but since all these qualities are invisible, you find them difficult to take in and make them your strength. You believe in what you can easily see, you then reflect on them, and they start appearing within you and increasing in your life.

For example, you see a huge flat-screen TV in your neighbor's house and you develop the desire: "I too should have this kind of TV." This thought is equivalent to a prayer and the process of its fulfilment begins and soon you find that type of TV in your house too. It is easy to bring the television into your reality because you had seen it, it was "real" to you; but to manifest that which is invisible requires power and deep contemplation. That's the purpose of *satsang*. When you listen to the truth and reflect on it, the invisible acquires the power to manifest.

Therefore, the highest decision in life is to always continue with *satsang* where you can continue listening to the truth.

Seeker: Is it possible to reach the heights of devotion in this materialistic world?

Sirshree: Valleys exist only where there are heights. This world has valleys, so that looking at those, one can aspire to reach the heights. Valleys put the heights into context. This world is like a classroom where you need to experiment with devotion. *For reaching the heights of devotion, you must enter the safe environment of service of the truth (seva).* This includes rendering service according to the teachings and instructions of your Guru.

For any scientific experiment, you need a lab. Likewise, for an experiment upon devotion, you need to go into the lab of service. When you carry out certain experiments in service, you would understand what are the heights and thereby you would be able to reach them. Hence, it won't be wrong to state that for attaining the heights of devotion, this material world is the best path.

4

Levels of Devotion

Seeker: How do I know where I have reached in my spiritual journey? If my devotion is the indication, then are there grades or levels in devotion?

Sirshree: First, it is important to look within and not look around to compare your journey with that of others. Each one's own journey is unique, and so is yours. Also remember that devotion is not just a path, but also an end in itself.

When you study in school, you pass through various grades till you reach the culmination of your education. Similarly, one ascends through broadly ten levels of devotion to finally attain God.

At each level of devotion, the state of the seeker is different. Therefore, the effort they put in varies according to their current understanding and level of maturity. Each successive level brings them closer to God. The purer their devotion, the quicker they unite with God.

The disposition of the seeker decides their level. So, let's take a look at the various levels.

Level 1: Blind Devotion

At level 1, devotion is blind, as it does not have the eye of understanding. The seekers blindly follow ritual mongers who confuse them with various rituals, rosaries, offerings, giving of alms, wearing religious robes, giving up worldly obligations, and so forth. They get entangled in various beliefs and dwell in the imagination of the joys of heaven. For them, devotion is more of an entertainment in the form of songs and dance; it is shallow and short-lived. Such seekers are not truly devotees; they may appear to be so from their external appearance but internally they follow their selfish agenda.

When devotion arises from blind faith and ignorance, it wavers in the face of adversities. The devotee's faith vacillates due to lack of understanding of truth. Such devotees have to come out of this stupor to progress on their journey. They have to listen to the truth, read, and contemplate the truth. As they gain understanding, they ascend to the second level of devotion.

Level 2: Karmic Devotion

When a seeker begins to understand how everything is a game of karma, their devotion rises to the second level. Their devotion hinges around the cycle of their karma and its fruit. When they understand that they reap the fruit of their actions—both good and bad—they start performing virtuous deeds and refrain from evil. This is beneficial for them.

Devotion at this stage also takes the form of repentance for bad deeds of the past. The seeker feels adulation for God, thinking that God has showered so much grace despite all their past sins. They repent and intend to make up for those sinful actions. At this stage, seekers believe that their present life is the fruit of karma from previous births; that God maintains an account of their sins and virtues, and that they get only what is in their destiny. They do not reflect on more fundamental questions such as: If our current birth is due to our actions in previous births, then due to which actions was our first birth?

Thus, at this level, one's actions are fruit-oriented and with the understanding that "I am responsible for my karma." It is good that one learns to take responsibility for one's actions, but there is also a risk at this level. When they succeed in performing good deeds, they admire their own actions and receive respect and praise. This can feed their ego, which reduces their possibility of reaching God. On the other hand, if they fail and perform bad deeds, they may curse their destiny.

Level 3: Devotion to Multiple Gods

Although the seeker believes in the concept of karma and its fruit, some questions begin to arise: Who gives us the fruit of our actions? Who decides which fruit should be given and when? As these questions gain depth, the seeker's desire for answers intensifies and they reach the third level of devotion.

After contemplating and seeking opinions of others, they begin to believe in God in the various manifold forms or deities. Due to beliefs prevalent since ancient times, people believe there are many different Gods. This practice continues even today—with people worshipping different deities that are believed to fulfill different wishes.

The seekers selectively worship various deities to address their personal needs. Their devotion takes the form of transactions. In return for their devotion, they expect God to fulfill their wishes. Their devotion is thus conditional. If they don't get what they desire after worshipping one deity, they shift to another.

For a seeker at this level of devotion, God means idols and images that represent various deities. Forms were conceived only to convey the formless essence. However, they miss this point and engage in idol worship. They also get entangled in rituals and beliefs surrounding the deities.

Each deity is believed to be pleased by certain acts and angered by certain other acts. For example, if a seeker observes a fast to please a deity, and if he happens to break the fast before the prescribed time, then he believes that the deity would be displeased with him. If he has a haircut on a particular day or eats a certain food item on a particular day on which it is prohibited, then he fears the wrath of a particular deity.

Thus, at this level, the seeker believes that there are many Gods and also drifts away from the main purpose of devotion.

Level 4: Singular Devotion

Assuming God to be manifold, seekers pray to different Gods, but when they don't get the fruit of their prayers, their faith in God diminishes. After being subject to such disillusionment, seekers enter the fourth level of devotion, where their understanding matures further.

They begin to realize that God may have various forms in the form of multiple deities, and God may be called by different names all around the world like Allah, Ishwar, Lord, Higher Self, etc. but there is essentially only one God. All prayers ultimately reach only one source.

At this level, the devotee prays knowing God to be the one source of everything. They thus prepare to shift their focus from the numerous forms to the formless, infinite, and absolute God. This can be called singular devotion. Their fear of God is replaced by love and reverence.

Seeker: How can someone who has grown up with fear of God's wrath shift to love for God? Also, does this mean various idols and rituals have no meaning?

Sirshree: Idols were originally created by some enlightened souls who wanted to visually express the Self that they were experiencing. They tried to give a form to the formless in their bliss and devotion. Various characteristics of the idols was a way to represent the attributes of the Self. However, we miss the point if we take a particular idol and think this is exactly how God looks like, and that others who consider other idols or the formless as God are wrong.

Idols do play an important role in the spiritual journey. In the initial stages, a seeker may not be able to fathom the formless, and hence a form can assist in beginning the journey. *Idols also help the restless mind to focus on God, and so do rituals. When you focus on the idol and contemplate the divine attributes, those attributes will start germinating within you*, since it is the law of nature that you attract what you focus on. Additionally, you may also remember the fact that you too are an idol created by God! All the crores of deities that are worshipped in India were actually symbolic of all the people that existed at the time the concept of deities was created, to indicate that God resides in everyone.

Seeker: Whoa! That's absolutely amazing. So, idol worship and rituals are very important.

Sirshree: They are important upto a point. Let's understand some more about their role through an analogy.

Suppose a child is scared of going into a dark alley and if you ask him to be bold and make use of his inner inspiration, he will find it difficult to understand your advice. If you were to preach to him saying, "Look here, my child, your thoughts and beliefs are baseless. When you watch horror movies, you experience fright and anxiety. It is thoughts that are responsible for your fears. There is actually nothing to fear in the dark alley." Such words will be beyond the understanding of the child. Instead, if the child is told, "If you wear this talisman, the ghosts that you fear will run away from you," he will definitely understand this.

The person who is giving the talisman knows that although it's merely a temporary remedy for the child's fear, it is necessary to change the child's thoughts at that time. After wearing the talisman, the child is not scared and feels certain that ghosts will never come close to him. He is able to go around anywhere without fear.

Having realized the importance of the talisman, the child will not be willing to cast it away. The permanent remedy for his fears is entirely different, but he is not able to comprehend this fact. But when he grows up and happens to go around even without the talisman, he realizes that his fears were baseless. He then gets rid of his fears and even understands the reason why the talisman was necessary during his childhood.

What has happened in spirituality is quite similar to this story. The practice of rituals that is imparted to the common man is merely a ladder on the way to the next level. However, people get stuck with rituals out of fear of displeasing an angry God. They believe in God in various forms; hence they are not prepared to comprehend God as the formless essence.

Consider an athlete who performs pole-vaulting. The pole propels him to a sufficient height so that he can vault across the horizontal bar. However, though the pole is useful in propping him to the required height, he has to leave the pole to cross over the bar. Imagine what will happen if he holds onto the pole and refuses to let it go.

Likewise, people are unwilling to leave the pole of rituals and idol worship by considering the superficial fears and benefits. The reality is that they can transcend all beliefs and vault across to the formless truth beyond all beliefs and rituals, only if they leave the pole.

However, at this level of devotion, *people refuse to cast aside their preconceived notions of karma and destiny, heaven and hell, and so forth. It is only after they get ready to leave the support of rituals and listen to the truth that they move to the next level of devotion.*

Though the idea of rituals may sound good, it is imperative that we go beyond rituals in order to attain the truth.

Seeker: Oh, now I understand, but people can spend their entire lifetime stuck in the web of superstitions and rituals. How can devotion grow out of these limitations in the lives of such people?

Sirshree: This can happen by the grace of a true guru.

Seeker: What is actually the role of a guru?

Sirshree: We can understand this by considering the next level of devotion.

Level 5: Devotion for the Guru

At the fifth level, the seeker's desire to know God, or the supreme truth, is awakened. They realize that the right guidance is essential to attain the truth. Only a living Guru can provide the right guidance; hence the seeker sets out in search of the Guru with great thirst in their heart. When a seeker is ready, the Guru appears in their life. After meeting the Guru and attaining supreme knowledge from the Guru, the seeker realizes that the final truth or God can be attained only by the grace of the Guru. *By the grace of God, one meets the Guru, and by the grace of the Guru, one meets God.*

As Saint Kabir has said, *"Guru Gobind dono khade, kaake laagun paaye? Balihari Guru aapno Gobind diyo milaye."* This means God and Guru are both standing before me, whom should I bow to first? I first bow to my Guru because it's due to him that I have met God.

(51) The seeker gradually begins to realize that *the Guru is not just a body, but is indeed the Self. The Guru's external body merely serves as an instrument for the Guru, God, or Self to awaken within us.* When this understanding deepens, it gives rise to a deep feeling of gratitude and devotion for the Guru. The seeker begins to follow all the instructions of the Guru.

(52) *The instructions of the Guru are meant to make the seeker's mind steady, pure, and loving. When seekers abide by the Guru's guidance, their life begins to be filled with wonder, bliss, and praise. They get liberated from all kinds of sorrows, vices, and problems by the Guru's grace.*

Every devotee needs to understand that each action of the Guru is meant for uplifting them. The Guru is the only one who speaks to you knowing who you really are. You have misunderstood your identity and assume yourself to be the body. Hence, you mistake the Guru as well to be an individual body.

The Guru speaks to you not with the intention of pleasing you, but to hurt you with love, so as to awaken you. This is the Guru's grace. The mind can never understand grace. It therefore imagines grace in its own terms. The Guru's presence will break all such false imaginations. There cannot be a greater grace in life than to be available in the presence of the Guru.

When the seeker recognizes this grace, their devotion soars. Devotion for the Guru then becomes more powerful in them than their strongest vice. This is the most auspicious state, as it opens the doors to enlightenment.

Level 6: Divine Devotion

In the beginning, a seeker prays to God to achieve their selfish ends. One may desire health, wealth, success, one may long for a spouse or an offspring, freedom from sorrows and worries, and so on. This is known as materialistic devotion. The devotee needs to climb out of the trench of materialistic devotion and reach the heights of divine devotion. After the devotee receives the final understanding of truth from the Guru at the fifth level, they attain divine devotion at the sixth level.

At this level of devotion, the devotee is liberated from all desires except for the single auspicious desire, which is expressed in the feeling: "Dear God… enough of this endless pursuit of material objects. None of the worldly pleasures can satisfy me any longer. Now I will be satisfied only after attaining You… You and only You!" With this feeling, they pray to God from the depths of their heart.

A mother caresses her baby and gives it some toys so that the baby can stay away from her for some time and play with the toys. Engrossed in those toys, the baby does forget the mother for some time. But after playing for some time, the baby pushes aside all the toys and starts crying for its mother. The mother has to then leave everything aside and come to the child.

In the same way, at the sixth level, the devotee gets fed up of the toys of illusion and resolves that they want only God, nothing less. They thereby ascend to the seventh level of devotion.

Level 7: Divine Submission Devotion

There was a poor villager, who was a sincere devotee of Lord Ganesha. He would eat only after offering food to the Lord. One day, he left for another village for some work. He carried along some jaggery just in case if he felt hungry during the short journey. On the way, when it was time for his daily worship, he started looking out for a temple of Lord Ganesha, but could not find one anywhere. He then got an idea and made a miniature idol of Ganesha from the jaggery he was carrying. Having used up all the jaggery to make the idol, he had nothing left to offer to the idol. He then pinched out some jaggery from the idol itself and offered the same back to it.

Thus, whatever was taken from God was returned to God. What we understand from this story can be expressed in the feeling, "Dear God... all this was always Yours, and is dedicated to You." This implies that there is nothing which is 'mine.' Everything belongs to God and is part of God. An individual makes various offerings such as fruits, flowers, wealth, various objects, service, etc. to God. When they attain the understanding that whatever they are offering to God already belongs to God and is part of God, then their ego begins to melt with the feeling of devotion.

This understanding continues to deepen until one fine day they realize, *"The one who is making the offerings—I—also belongs to God and is part of God." With this understanding, the ego, which was surviving based on an assumed separateness from God, surrenders.* The feeling of a separate 'I' that appeared due to ignorance of the truth vanishes. Devotion takes the form of divine submission and the mind experiences the joy of bowing down for the first time. The mind stops taking credit for all the work that was done in the past, or is being done in the present, or that will be done in the future.

When devotion of this level awakens within the devotee, they experience true joy, which then strengthens the spirit of surrender in them. They realize that they have done absolutely nothing to gain the blessings which they have received; it is simply the grace of God.

Level 8: Divine Acceptance Devotion

The underlying desire of a devotee is to attain the supreme truth or God. Though this is an auspicious and sacred desire, yet it is a desire. At the eighth level, the devotee gives up even this desire. They know that they will have no complaint and their love for God will remain unchanged even if they cannot attain God. They have surrendered even their highest desire. This is the state of ultimate acceptance.

For the devotee who has ascended such heights of devotion, it can indeed be very painful to accept that they may not attain the truth after all. On the other hand, when this becomes totally acceptable to them, then the attainment of truth becomes very easy. However, if the devotee tries to short-circuit the process by giving up the desire for truth believing that they can then attain the truth, then this is not acceptance; it is ignorance. If there is the slightest trace of greed in the feeling of acceptance, then it is not acceptance at all. Hence, it is important that the feeling of acceptance arises from sincerity and understanding.

When the devotee begins to understand the truth through direct experience of the true self, divine acceptance devotion begins. With this devotion, the devotee is in the spirit of 'Bright acceptance;' they have risen beyond the feelings of acceptance and non-acceptance. They accept their acceptance as well as their non-acceptance, if any. There is no resistance in their mind to any situation. As the feeling of total acceptance and surrender keeps rising with devotion, so does their joy. It is true joy, which springs from the Source within and not due to any external reason.

At this level, it does not take any effort for the devotee to reach the next level and they automatically ascend to the ninth level.

Level 9: Divine Wisdom Devotion

At the ninth level, all the secrets of the Creator and its Creation are unveiled and the devotee experiences oneness with God, just like a river that merges into the ocean. This is self-realization, God-realization, attainment of the supreme truth.

The devotee understands that there was always only One; they realize the divine play that was going on—that it is God who was seeking Himself by becoming a separate devotee.

It is in this state that the illusion is dispelled and the truth manifests. The devotee becomes free from duality—free from the opposites of joy and sorrow, success and failure, honor and dishonor, life and death, you and I.

When a seeker begins the journey with wisdom, their search culminates in devotion. In the same way, the devotee who begins the journey with devotion ultimately attains wisdom.

With this wisdom, one becomes a true devotee, ever-immersed in the bliss of devotion. Thus, when the devotee attains the truth, there is blending of wisdom and devotion.

This experience cannot be expressed in words. It can only be known through experience, as it is beyond the realms of the body, mind, and intellect. The body just becomes the means to experience this state. *Just as the mirror is a medium for the eye to see itself, God uses the body of the pure devotee as a clean mirror to experience Oneself.*

Level 10: Bright Divine Devotion

When the devotee and God become one, then what remains to be done?! Hence, at the tenth level, the devotee and God once again become two from one! This is a matter of great depth.

After becoming a devotee once again, they begin to experience amazement due to the various things that begin to manifest in their life so easily. They now have the divine eye to witness the wonders of the world, just like a child who is struck by wonder and joy. With the awakening of Bright divine devotion, they begin to observe these wonders while being established in the Self. This astonishment is not the mind's invention; rather it is the state that results after dissolution of the dual mind.

Suppose a father and daughter are playing a game of hide-and-seek. The father hides and the daughter is searching the whole house for him. When she is unable to find him even after searching for a long time, she begins to cry. On hearing her cry, her father suddenly appears before her. You can imagine the feelings of the child at this juncture. The fright at her father's sudden appearance, the wonder of having spotted him, and the joy of seeing him again are all mixed together.

Now the girl tells her father, "You go and hide once more. I will again search for you." Hereafter, the girl enjoys the game, as she now has the conviction that her father can never be lost to her. The search for him is simply for enjoyment. The father hides once more, the daughter searches for him again, and he again appears suddenly. Instead of fear, now she experiences a bliss of a different kind.

This state cannot be defined in words. *The devotee and God become one and then separate only for feeling even more joy; this is when Bright divine devotion begins—a state which is beyond devotion and non-devotion.*

These are the ten levels of devotion that one ascends in this journey. After understanding the levels of devotion, it's now time to ask yourself, "Where is my devotion today? How can I raise my level?" If you really wish to realize God and be established in that sublime experience, then you need to deeply contemplate each of these levels. Only devotion can help you to unite with God.

Seeker: Wow! What an amazing and beautiful journey!

Sirshree: Indeed. The journey of God finding God. That's why it's called *lila*—the divine game.

5

Principles of Devotion

Seeker: Are there any principles of devotion, just as there are of knowledge? If yes, what are they?

Sirshree: There are two principles of devotion that need to be understood. If you can have faith in them, then you would never have to be afraid of anything in the world. You might have heard of them before, but wouldn't have thought of them in this way. Probably you believe in them but lack total conviction. So, understand them and develop complete conviction.

First principle of devotion is: Everything is in God's hands.

Most people believe in this principle. *Yes, everything is in the Lord's hands. So, then?* Then only one point is left. If you can also believe in the second principle, there is absolutely no problem in life. However, this belief has to be accompanied by understanding. Otherwise, it is very easy to simply say that you agree.

Second principle of devotion is: God makes no mistakes.

God can never make any mistake. If you agree, then what does it mean? It means that if you agree, then it's not a mistake. If you don't agree, it's still not a mistake because God does not make mistakes. If God does everything and if God makes no mistakes, then what's left?

Then whatever happens in your life, you will say to yourself, *"It's God's doing and God makes no mistakes." If you are convinced in the truth of this principle, you will say this in every situation. If you are not, then there is much to complain about and there are a lot of questions.* "Why this, why that? God, why are you doing this?" But even this is not a mistake. Because God wants you to complain and criticize. Whatever happens, it's His will. If He did not want it to happen, you would not have complained in the first place. Also, if you are criticizing, it is because He wants you to be empty. You are doing it because of emotions built up inside you. After complaining, you feel better. Be convinced from within that this is true, that this is necessary. This is designed by God, so it is needed. Maybe you will realize this now, or a few years later, or in the afterlife—that there are no mistakes.

But when this complaining occurs, ask yourself if you recall the principles of devotion. Are you aware of the truth? When people criticize, they forget the truth. People get entangled in the web spun by their own words. These two principles of devotion are the answer.

For the devotee, these principles work like magic. Whatever is happening, with regards to work, marriage, children, relations, health, or regarding any adverse situation in life, they have faith that it is in God's hands and God does not make mistakes. Then the devotee abides in devotion and the state of devotion propels them joyfully across the ocean of life. The intellectual also crosses the ocean but not with the same enjoyment. The devotee experiences a deep joy in life. This is the beauty of devotion, because devotion is somehow close to the love of this world. Every human being wants to experience love. Love can be experienced in devotion, so it is closer to the heart. *In this world, where love gets transformed into attachment and sorrow, devotion gives a glimpse of true love which liberates you.* The only danger is that infatuation or attachment is mistaken as true love, and hence, knowledge is also necessary.

Check, "Is devotion flowing in my life? Has this devotion arisen from knowledge and understanding? Do I merely believe in the principles of devotion or do I know these to be the final truth? Do I even remember them during most situations in my life? When undesirable events take place, it doesn't even occur to me that this cannot be a mistake."

Knowledge and devotion are the two wings that will enable you to fly. Hence, do not neglect either.

Seeker: How can a devotee remain happy and content?

Sirshree: How do devotees think and how do they call the Lord? How is their devotion so innocent? Bhakt Prahlad is remembered during the festival of Holi. There is an innocence in his devotion. He sits in the lap of the terrifying Hiranyakashyap because it's his father. Everyone else is afraid of the heinous demon. But the devotee Prahlad looks innocently at the horrendous face, because he is free of any preconceived notions. Most of us have these notions that this face is pretty and that face is horrible. When you can keep all these notions aside and appreciate the presence of God in all faces, because you have attained knowledge and also the innocence of devotion, then you can remain happy and content everywhere.

(61) A devotee says, *"Don't say that your problems are big. Tell your problems that your God is bigger—in fact bigger than all the problems put together."* This will fill you with hope, faith, and strength. The error we are all making is we are considering our problems to be bigger than God, which creates sorrow and misery.

So, what is innocent devotion? Being without preconceived notions. A devotee has the strength to move mountains. Their strength lies in their faith. There is contentment in their love. (62) *Faith is a devotee's strength and love is their contentment.*

Everyone craves for this contentment, satisfaction, or fulfilment. People keep searching for this satisfaction in all possible ways, but they remain unquenched. Suppose someone craves for position and power, and strives day and night for it. When he finally gets it, if he is truly honest, he will admit that he is still not content. When someone runs behind wealth and attains it, yet they don't feel content. Someone desires a bungalow and achieves it. After some time, ask them if they feel totally fulfilled? No. Someone wants a swanky car and manages to get one. Before getting it, they thought that something special was going to happen. After all the running around, when they finally get the car, how long do they remain happy? Again, some discontent is felt. Now they want a son or a daughter. After that happens, does the satisfaction last? The happiness quickly fades away after getting the desired object; there is no lasting contentment.

Then how is this contentment actually found? All this running around is happening for finding lasting peace. Man is deluded if he thinks that contentment is just around the corner, in the next thing. Because it never is. And then he comes upon the *bhakti sutra* or the next principle of devotion.

Seeker: What is that bhakti sutra?

Sirshree: This bhakti sutra says that there is something within us that has never felt any sorrow, any lack, or discontentment. That 'something' abides in unconditional love and causeless bliss. It dwells in joy with or without the presence of any position, power, spouse, children, or any reason under the sun. That something is our real self. Recognizing our relation to that thing, to our real self, is devotion.

What is needed to have a relationship with it? Devotion. And what is needed for increasing devotion? Relationship with it. A relationship is formed by meeting it, again and again. Meetings make a relationship. You can meet it by taking a dip within and experiencing it. These dips give you glimpses of your true nature, and this deepens your devotion.

The unconditional love and bliss is always present within you. It has not gone anywhere. It is simply covered with karmic bondages. These bondages can be broken by asking forgiveness from the depth of your heart. As the bondages break, the love and bliss open up layer by layer. And when you ponder upon them, they bloom. When you talk about them or listen about them, they open. So, if you want to deepen this relationship, devotion is required. If this is clear, you will progress easily.

You may feel that your preconceived notions are a hurdle. Then you will get rid of those notions. You will stop being driven by those notions. You will go back to a child-like innocence. Jesus said that those who are like children will inherit the kingdom of heaven. We have to enter the kingdom of heaven within us, because we need to form a solid relationship with it. Only love can make this relationship happen. Spouting knowledge is not going to do it. Nor will position, power, or wealth. *It takes innocent devotion to gain access and abide in the heaven within.*

This is a huge task, but worth the introspection, the inner work. We must ask ourselves, why do we feel that it is necessary to manipulate, to be clever, and lie to people to get our work done? Why do we hold on to the belief that we will not succeed if we don't cheat each other? Then we also teach our children that they will have to adopt unfair means to succeed. However, the fact is that we can create our reality with our thoughts. God has given us the law of love, the laws of thought, and the law of karma.

If you are aware of these laws, you will always confidently march towards your progress. Even if the outer reality seems to tell you that something is wrong, you will remain steadfast in your conviction on the bhakti sutras, and very soon, the clouds will part and the sun will shine its glory upon you. And for this, you will have to walk on the path of innocence.

Seeker: What are the other obstacles to surrendering on the path of devotion?

Sirshree: An individual's doubts about God and the nature of God can become an obstacle. Preconceived notions and ideas about God are hurdles too. These notions have to be removed. Only then does devotion become pure and innocent, which helps in surrendering.

A child is so very innocent. It's a joy to listen to a child, because they don't speak from preconceived notions. They say whatever they understand or see in the situation. Likewise, *when a devotee regards the Lord with innocence and purity, the Lord appears and the individual disappears.* Hence, you have to ask yourself whether your devotion is such that the Lord will appear to you. Otherwise, it will just become blind devotion or devotion that provides some temporary relief.

Seeker: Are there any other principles of devotion described by other saints?

Sirshree: Yes, many saints have expressed the principles of devotion in different ways. One of the principles in the words of Shri Ramakrishna Paramhansa is: "I am the machine and He is the operator. I am the house and He is the dweller. It is my right to render service as ordained by Him."

According to this principle, the body is simply an instrument, which is operated by God. The devotee should perform actions in the spirit of service. As long as you harbor the notions of a separate "me" and "you," you get stuck in this illusion of separateness. If you serve God with the spirit of service and surrender, you can get liberated.

Shri Ramakrishna also said, "If one sheds tears on hearing the name of God, know for certain that this is their last birth before they dwell in life immortal." Some people may find it difficult to agree with this because their intellectual bent of mind does not easily accept this. But had the same thing been said by a scientist, they would immediately buy into it. But those, who have tasted the nectar of true devotion and dwell in the experience of divine *being*, will immediately understand this.

For those who could not immerse themselves in devotion, Shri Ramakrishna said, "Individuals who harbor emotions like shame, hatred, and fear, can neither surrender nor attain God. Even though divine attainment is possible, they keep worrying about what their family and others will say. They also fear that if they go ahead in life as per God's orders, then who will take care of their personal needs and what will happen to them."

One becomes a true devotee only when one completely surrenders to God, leading to the dissolution of ego.

6

Receptivity and Miracles in Devotion

Seeker: What is the meaning of receptivity?

Sirshree: If it so happens that as soon as you think something, you start feeling it, and then immediately it translates into action from the Self—then that's receptivity. This happens because you are connected to the Self; you are the Self. If the 'separate individual' is in between, it prevents things from arising from the Self. As soon as the 'individual' moves aside, you align with the Self and become receptive to it.

With receptivity, a single thought will attune you to the Self or the Source, and you instantly start feeling it and easily act on it. This is amazing and astonishing. What an individual is unable to think and do in several years, starts happening so effortlessly. This is the power of devotion.

This connecting with the Self or opening of the heart occurs with devotion. Otherwise, you may grapple with the issue of how your heart can open. The heart cannot open if you live in your head all the time. You have to come down to the heart. It's a fine line. If you can grasp it—it's eureka. You are lucky if you can achieve such receptivity that wherever you are, you just get a thought and the right decisions and actions begin to arise from within you. If the 'individual' would have battled the same issue with the mind, it wouldn't have got the answer or the solution. This is the important thing to note about receptivity.

Seeker: What is the importance of receptivity in devotion?

Sirshree: Devotion is something that cannot be imbibed with just words, hence you have to cultivate receptivity. If you become receptive, it's a miracle. The transfer of devotion is a miracle. It takes place by becoming receptive and open, because divine grace is ever present and always showering on everyone. People are not receptive for it. *Those who are receptive come and attend a discourse in the Guru's presence. Devotion gets transferred, the teaching is received, and their life is transformed.* It all depends upon receptivity.

Simply attending a retreat or discourse is not enough. Don't be under the misconception that your spiritual retreat is done, unless the essence of the teaching and the devotion is transferred within you.

Being receptive in the Guru's presence is what creates the Upanishads. When a disciple became receptive, the questions emerged from the tejasthan (heart or center) of the disciple and answers from the Guru's tejasthan. When these were recorded, an Upanishad (sacred text) came into being.

So, you need to be present and receptive, then whatever arises will do its work. *You have to be receptive during the discourse, and then continue that receptivity even outside in the world. If you are able to do that, you will receive the supreme truth and get established in it. If not, then there is still work to be done.* Sometimes you experience devotion during the discourses or retreats, but forget about it later on. Hence, your devotion should first intensify during discourses, so that even when you are outside, you will remember it and immediately shift back to devotion. Thus, your devotion should be not just during session but in action too.

Seeker: What is *bhakti yog*?

Sirshree: You meet so many different people. You may have noticed that if you meet happy people, their happiness gets transferred and you feel happy too. That's why you feel like meeting someone joyful, especially when you are feeling low. At that time, you visit someone who is the happiest according to you. That individual may be happy because things are working out his way, or all is going well in his life, or he may have decided to be happy no matter what. Then *there is another kind of happiness that is radiated by someone who is established in the supreme truth. Coming in contact with this kind of joy is called as 'bhakti yog.'*

We get connected to the place from where the divine essence is being transmitted. That's why it is called grace. And that's why a Guru is so important. *A Guru can be considered as an open safe. Being in his/her presence automatically starts opening the closed safe of your heart too.* Thereby you connect with the Self and the bliss.

Seeker: When we read the stories of saints, it seems their lives are full of miracles. What is the science behind these miracles? How can miracles occur in our life?

Sirshree: What exactly is a miracle? When you are about to lose something and then at the last moment that something is revived, you call it a miracle.

According to the level of the listeners and to maintain liveliness, stories are often presented in an embellished and metaphorical manner: poisoning, getting trampled by elephants, thrown among hungry lions, tossed in fire, pushed down a mountain… but devotees like Bhakt Prahlad, Mira or Kabir emerge unscathed from such catastrophes in a miraculous manner. Be it Socrates or Sita, they easily passed their tests, without feeling any heat of the fires they were subjected to.

When people listen to the miracles described in these stories, they believe that God showered special grace on those great devotees during those events, in the form of divine light that saved them from any harm. An individual with an ordinary intellect cannot understand the real message hidden in these stories. He thinks that similar miracles will happen with him too. As a result, his devotion towards God is due to the belief that miracles will occur in his life as well. When that doesn't happen, he turns away from devotion.

The reality is that miracles occur when one is a true devotee. Those saints were true devotees of God. Because of real devotion, they were automatically trained as to where their attention should be focused during adverse circumstances: not on the circumstance itself, but on their center or tejasthan (*tejasthan* is the place roughly in the region of the heart where the Universal Self connects with the body). They did not waver and remained established in the experience of Self. Hence, adversities came and went, but they remained untouched.

Some people get trained by applying consistent efforts; whereas due to devotion, devotees get automatically trained while facing the events of life. In the presence and by the guidance of the Guru, many disciples become devotees but they do not become true devotees. True devotees are those who have unconditional devotion and are always aligned with and operate from their center. Let us look at a story through which we will understand the role of these factors.

Once upon a time there lived a king who sometimes used to walk about in his country in ordinary attire, so that he could check upon his kingdom unrecognized. He once came upon a man who used to make pots during the day, sing hymns joyously before bed, and then sleep peacefully.

The King wondered how this poor man managed to be so happy. He did not possess any wealth, nor did he have any security for the future, but seemed unconcerned by it. So, the King started a conversation with the potter and asked the secret of his happiness. The potter said, "Well, what's there to be worried about? I make pots and sell them, there's enough money for food. When there is extra money, I even feed one more person. So, life's good."

The King decided to test him, and arranged it so that the potter did not get food. But the man was still happy. After four such instances of forced fasting, when the potter was still happy, the

King lost patience and got the potter to enlist in the army to make a living. Within a few days, the potter was given the task of beheading a criminal.

The potter started praying from the bottom of his heart. "Oh God! I don't want to be the cause of this man's death. Please help me. If you don't want me to do this, please turn my sword into a wooden one." Everyone was listening to the prayer, including the King. The potter pulled out his sword from the sheath and everybody's mouth fell open. It was a wooden sword! The King was astounded by this miracle. He confessed the entire truth and rewarded him handsomely. The potter returned home and happily narrated the event to his wife.

His wife couldn't remain silent and she in turn confessed that the children had been hungry since two days and hence she had sold the sword and bought some food. She had replaced it with their kids' wooden sword, so that he won't come to know.

How would we have remembered this story, if the wife hadn't told the truth? Thus, each and every thought is connected; it's miraculous who is given which thought. The King had to test the potter, the potter had to pray aloud, and the wife had to change the sword.

These stories demonstrate that *only if one is aligned with Self, then events unfold in miraculous ways. We feel surprised thinking how did this happen.* One never knows what thought might be given and what might get done. Hence, always wish well for others, so that you are always in alignment with Self. Pray for every person, "You are sacred and divine. May you always be happy." Keep doing this and you will be surprised with miracles in your life. But don't engage in devotion for miracles. The ultimate goal of devotion is much higher. Miracles just occur in the process.

Seeker: How is the way of the heart (devotion) unique from that of using our body, mind, or intellect for attaining the truth?

Sirshree: Let's consider a little story.

Four boys from a village were seeking a very famous pearl guarded by a serpent. The pearl was on the other side of a huge and tumultuous river. The boys were determined to get the pearl and started their preparation in earnest.

The first boy began exercising his muscles, and though he could swim, he began practicing it vigorously. His idea was that he would need strong muscles and better swimming prowess to be able to swim across. He also started to learn to play the snake charmer's flute so that he could charm the snake.

The second boy began building a boat and weaving a basket. His plan was to build a boat to get to the other side, ensnare the snake in the basket, and capture the pearl.

The third boy's method was simpler. He befriended a boatman, who was a master in both navigating the river as well as handling snakes. They began the journey right away to get across, and during the journey, the boy started learning how to navigate the river and how to charm snakes from the boatman.

The fourth boy sat down at the shore of the river and all he did was pray to the serpent with all his heart. Lo and behold! The serpent carried the pearl across the river and laid it as his feet.

The boys represent various types of seekers, the snake is symbolic of *maya* or the illusory world, and the pearl is God or supreme truth. Each of these methods reminds us of four different ways to attain the truth. The first is the physical way or using the body to reach the truth. Second method is intellectual, third is mental, and fourth is that of the heart or devotion.

True and deep devotion directly connects you to the Self. Even the illusory world reminds you of truth and helps you to attain the truth when you are in devotion. Thus, devotion can bring forth the pearl of truth in your life in a way unlike any other. It's unique and incredible.

7

Deepening the Practice of Devotion

Seeker: Why is it that some people can easily develop devotion, while others cannot?

Sirshree: Let us consider an analogy to understand the reason.

Imagine there are five different earthen pots before you. Some of these pots are kept upside down and some are kept upright. These pots are symbolic of individuals with different dispositions. Let us see what happens when one tries to fill the pots with the color of devotion (water which is colored in devotion).

POT 1: When one tries to pour the color of devotion into the first pot, the color cannot enter it because it is kept upside down. This symbolizes a person who is not open or receptive. These individuals do not want to see the color nor acknowledge the emptiness within them. That is why even though the color of devotion was poured on them, it did not enter them because they were not receptive for it.

POT 2: In case of the second pot, the color of devotion cannot enter because it is already filled to its brim with liquor (symbolizing all vices and unconsciousness) so that there is no room for devotion.

POT 3: The third pot has many fissures and therefore whatever color is poured in this pot drains out. People with such mentality cannot hold the color of devotion in their hearts or minds because they entertain a lot of negative thoughts. They have doubts, arguments, and disagreements in their mind. Hence, they cannot easily receive devotion with an open mind. These people cannot even receive the blessings given to them because they are not receptive for them. They then complain that the Guru blessed everybody except them. The Guru then has to tell them, "Instead of getting upset and doubting the Guru, look at the holes in your pot. Look within and find out why your mind cannot retain any blessings."

These people want to be in devotion, they want the blessings, but their inner state contradicts what they want, and so there is a constant battle between "yes, I want this" and "but…." If there is a fissure in your pot, the Guru's blessings would drain out, no matter how quickly the pot is being filled.

(76) Thus, if your pot is kept upside down (unreceptive), if it is filled with liquor (vices and unconsciousness) or if it has holes (negativity, doubts, wrong beliefs, and faith only in rituals), then devotion cannot awaken within you.

(77) First appreciate the benefits of the blessings you have already received. If you fail to be grateful for what you have, you cannot be open to more of what you desire.

POT 4: The fourth pot is contaminated with poisonous algae. Even if nectar is poured in this pot, it becomes toxic. Whoever drinks the water from this pot would fall sick. People with such a poisonous mentality derive pleasure from hurting others. They always have evil thoughts about others, and they create problems for everyone. It's best to avoid the company of such people because otherwise their crooked mentality can affect you and poison your pot too.

POT 5: The fifth pot is kept upright and at the same time it is empty and pure. This denotes the individual who is open and not filled with wrong beliefs or negative tendencies. When the color of devotion is poured in them, they receive it openly and joyously. They get filled with devotion. With the power of devotion, the water in this pot will become nectar, and it would not only benefit them but others as well.

Please pause for a few minutes and reflect on this. Then ask yourself, "What is my pot like? What is the state of my mind? Is it receptive for devotion and blessings?"

You can be filled with devotion only if you are like the fifth pot—if your mind is pure and receptive for grace, then it is able to receive devotion.

The Guru blesses those who are not ready to surrender to devotion by placing his/her hand on the individual's head, so that this would bow down their head (which is symbolic of surrender). This is because you cannot attain unconditional devotion by remaining at the level of intellect, you need to get down from the head and remain at the heart or *tejasthan*.

Seeker: Various attractions in today's world make it difficult to tread the spiritual path. Can I really develop pure devotion in these conditions?

Sirshree: The illusory world can have a very strong hold over us. Something even stronger is needed to break this hold. *Devotion has that kind of strength which can help us override the attractions of this world.* In the earlier times, there were no smartphones or social media, and yet the worldly attraction was quite powerful. Today the situation is quite bad but the power of devotion can make it possible.

Surrender everything and pray, "Dear Lord, I want neither joy nor sorrow. Bless me with only pure devotion. I want neither good nor bad, just pure devotion." When you desire and implore for pure devotion, it can transform you.

When you listen to the stories of great souls, you will develop the conviction that pure devotion can be attained because they successfully achieved it. People have faced brutal conditions but responded with devotion and thus became ideals. So, it's possible for you too. Everyone has their own set of difficulties, but in spite of them, what is the least you can do? What's the minimum percent of devotion-filled response that you can give? This is how you have to think and act.

Seeker: How can devotion deepen?

Sirshree: Devotion begins with prayer. You communicate with God through prayer. You can pray, "Dear God, whenever I remember you, please immerse me in the experience of truth." Pray this repeatedly and with all your heart. Mother Nature observes you to see if you really want it or you forget all about it after praying just once. Hence, you should pray repeatedly and its intensity should increase. The feeling of devotion will begin.

Next is to praise God's attributes. You will be able to do this when you listen to stories of saints. The more you listen or read these stories, the more it will inspire devotion within you. *The more deeply the description of divine attributes reaches within you and you are able to understand them, the more your devotion blossoms.* The life stories of saints as well as stories of their devotees will raise your devotion. This is because they make you realize the height of the level of consciousness within them. The lives of Saint Meera or Sudama are wonderful inspirations for us. How did they become devotees? How were they before? Then what happened? How were they tested in devotion? How did the testing become tasty for them? How were they able to successfully pass that difficult phase?

Further on, in order to deepen your devotion, contemplate the stories created by the saints or enlightened ones. Profound truths were weaved into those stories, so that they could inspire devotion even after centuries. But today mostly people read them and forget them. Festivals were created by the enlightened ones for the same reason of propagating devotion and truth. If you celebrate Ganesh festival and then submerge the idol, what does it mean? The ego should be submerged and dissolve. This was the purpose of that festival. Feel the grace that they created such stories and traditions; allow the feeling of devotion to rise. The more you feel gratitude and grace, the more your devotion will deepen.

Real devotion means simply being present for the Self to express itself through your body. In that presence, if your ignorance, wrong beliefs, vices, and tendencies are dissolved, then it is the right presence. This presence is possible in inner silence, or in other words, meditation. That is why meditation should be a part of your daily routine. Instead of wasting your precious time indulging in vices and worldly tendencies, use your time wisely to reach the Self through the depths of meditation.

Continue to listen to the discourses of your master and read books containing the teachings. Contemplate in depth upon them, only then will those teachings permeate your life. Render service with the understanding that Self is serving the Self. This will prevent you from taking any credit or developing ego of service. This will deepen your devotion.

Devotion is going to benefit you because it will help you get rid of your tendencies, as it raises your awareness and capability.

Seeker: How does devotion increase our capability and awareness?

Sirshree: A devotee faithfully adheres to even seemingly trivial instructions of their master. What's the purpose of the Guru's instructions? The purpose is that your devotion should rise, so that your awareness increases. When you have devotion, you become aware and alert to ensure that you are following even the smallest instructions and not doing anything wrong. Otherwise, people make grave mistakes in their lives without ever thinking whether they are doing something wrong.

With devotion, an awareness starts building up that extends

to every aspect of life. For instance, if the tap is running while brushing your teeth, you will become aware of this and the small effort of turning it off will start occurring naturally. This awareness will build up to reach the subtle levels and you become capable of grasping the subtle feeling of your *being*. You need training for grasping subtle things. Nobody gives you such training, but devotion does this job. *You may or may not have been responsible till now; devotion brings on this responsibility. After the commencement of devotion, in every situation, the thought arises, "What would God want in this situation? How should I fulfill God's will?"*

You have experienced that you've gained nothing by fulfilling the "individual's" will. With devotion, you will happily fulfill God's will. It's a bonus if your awareness increases. And that will in turn deepen your devotion even further, and you will start glorifying God.

Seeker: What are the various ways of glorifying God?

Sirshree: You can glorify God, or in other words practice devotion, in many different ways, such as singing hymns, dancing, letting tears flow in devotion, rendering service, or sitting in silence in meditation.

The purpose of our body-mind is to sing the glories of the Lord. The more clearly you understand this, the more you will be able to do it. Thereby you'll be able to use your body-mind for fulfilling your purpose on Earth.

Shri Ramakrishna has said that for a devotee, practicing devotion is akin to scratching an itch. The more you scratch, the more you feel like scratching. When devotees sing the glories of the Lord, they feel like going on and on. They never get tired of it. Unlimited energy seems to flow through them. These words sprung from his own experience.

Practice devotion with the clear understanding of why you have been given this body-mind? Why have you been given these eyes, ears, and tongue? Until you are totally convinced of this, you will continue to use your body-mind and sense organs for your individual desires and ambitions.

If a devotee wants more time, it's only for practicing devotion. If a devotee prays for health, it's only for practicing devotion. If a devotee eats or breathes, it's only for practicing devotion.

Seeker: Wow, that's deep! I have been wondering, is singing hymns an important part of devotion?

Sirshree: When spiritual wisdom as well as feelings towards God are weaved into just a few lines and sung immersed in deep feeling, it becomes a hymn. Hymns are a wonderful medium to express our feelings to God, and it's also an art. Great saints of India like Mira, Surdas, Guru Nanak, Kabir, and others used hymns to easily spread the intricate knowledge of spirituality to the common man.

Even today people are inspired by the hymns and poems of these saints, and move closer to God by listening to them. When devotees express their love, commitment, and surrender to God in the form of a hymn, people are forced to wonder about their exquisite state. "What is so special about devotion that this person looks so blissful?" They don't find such bliss in the material world, and therefore turn from the material world towards devotion to experience it.

The ego automatically begins to surrender when one sings hymns in true devotion, and hence hymns have been given so much importance till date. *If the ego surrenders, then the hymns have done their job; if not, then those hymns are merely entertainment or ego-boosters for the singer.*

Hymns are praise—praise of the glory of the Supreme Creator who created the universe, praise of the Self which is present in every being, and from whence all thoughts emerge like waves. A hymn has a direct correlation with one's feelings. With the help of a hymn, one may express one's yearning to meet God, while another may convey the joy of having met God. One may pray to God for cultivating good qualities, while another may remind people the foolishness of harboring ego since this life on Earth is just a temporary illusion.

The goal of devotion and hymns is to stabilize every devotee in the ultimate truth or God. Hymns and praises of God emerged from those who experienced the ultimate truth. Even if a movie song increases your understanding, then it is a hymn; and if a hymn reminds you of and stimulates your bad habits, then it's no good.

Seeker: How does devotion translate into our everyday life?

Sirshree: As much as possible, try to be in devotion every moment of your daily life. Otherwise, you will be inclined to make a big deal even out of minor incidents. Consequently, at that time, you forget that nature is testing you by creating a situation. *Always remember that nature puts you to the test time and time again, for the purpose of strengthening your devotion. With devotion, you give a positive response in spite of all that is going on around you. With a positive response, you overcome your tendencies. If you don't overcome your tendencies, they intensify and dominate you.*

Let purity become the tendency and habit of your mind. In divine devotion, your mind becomes pure. The bondages of karma begin to break and you will realize that happiness comes from within. If somebody tries to extract oil from sand, or milk from water, this effort is futile as there is no oil in sand or milk in water. In the same way, *trying to derive happiness by fulfilling the desires of the mind and the five senses, by giving in to the tendencies, is bound to be futile.* In fact, this is comparatively more terrible and meaningless, because by doing so, the tendencies get deeper.

The cause of bondage of karma is wrong tendencies. The karma in itself does not create the bondage. For example, if you slap somebody, it does not lead to any bondage. But if you develop the tendency of slapping, and your hand automatically rises to slap in every situation, then that is bondage. In most people, the tendency to use abusive words, steal things, etc. gets developed in this manner. This is bondage.

Most people are ignorant about this. That is why time and again people try to obtain happiness by indulging in pleasures of the senses. As a result, they develop the habit of getting entangled in their negative tendencies. Therefore, seekers of truth are cautioned to become aware of the trap of tendencies. For example, seekers are advised to avoid getting caught up in television or internet for deriving pleasure. If they get entangled, it becomes difficult to get rid of this tendency. Many people spend their whole life stuck in such bondages.

Additionally, people waste so much precious time running behind those pleasures. For instance, as soon as people feel even a little bored, they switch on the TV and spend hours watching it, without even realizing that they have squandered valuable time which they can never get back. Some people are extremely fond of food. They try to seek enjoyment in every restaurant. If they don't like the food in one restaurant, they search for another. This goes on. Over a period of time, this seemingly ordinary activity slowly turns into a tendency. Only devotion can help overcome such tendencies.

Many people try even harsh spiritual practices such as self-flagellation and starvation, in order to win over their mind, but they remain unsuccessful. Hence, you should prepare your mind with love and give it the sweet taste of devotion. *The mind becomes pure with devotion to God and its tendencies begin to dissolve. It then surrenders on its own. You win.*

Seeker: What is devotion-in-action?

Sirshree: *Devotion-in-action means doing sadhana or spiritual practice that the Guru has asked you to, no matter what.* Practice meditation and follow the commands of your Guru daily and without fail. Give the right response to the events occurring in your life. When you do this using dedication and common sense, it means your devotion has reached new heights and now it is seen in your actions. At this stage, you automatically say, "I have made a promise to my master and that's why now I won't even listen to my mind." That means you follow all the instructions of your master, without any excuses. If you fail to do this in certain situations, then next time see how you can do it. You would then be taking the right actions which are easily possible. This is the power of devotion.

Seeker: How can we give a devotion-filled response even when tendencies have arisen and are trying to compel us to give the opposite response?

Sirshree: As far as possible, you should try to give a devotion-filled response to every person and every situation. Try your best.

Always remember the words 'in spite of.' These words can arise only because of devotion, and they will always help you to give a devotion-filled response. For instance, if you are getting angry you can say, "I am feeling angry, but in spite of that, I will give a polite response." Make the words 'in spite of' a part of your plan to get rid of your tendencies. This will help to ignite the cool fire of devotion within you, which will burn and destroy all your bad tendencies and vices.

In the beginning, there is a constant conflict between your tendencies and devotion. There is the mind at one end which wants to drive you according to its own desires, and on the other end there is the thirst for truth that asks you to surrender to God. Which side would you like to win? If you have tasted devotion, then you would definitely go for devotion because you have understood that the supreme bliss you get by surrendering in devotion is not achieved by going the mind's way or by indulging in the illusion.

You would need to make some effort for devotion to win over your tendencies. One of the effort would be that you will have to develop awareness and observe the incidents occurring in your life throughout the day, to check where devotion wins and where tendencies win. Supposing 30 incidents—big, small, minor—take place on an average day. You observe yourself during those incidents and find that you gave a positive and devotion-filled response during 10 incidents. During another 10 incidents, your response was neutral, i.e. at that time there was neither devotion nor any tendency. During the remaining 10 incidents, your response was driven by ego and the whims of the mind.

Now if you reflect on the last type of incidents, and work consistently to change your response, gradually you will find that the number of your tendencies reduces with time, and one day you will give a devotion-filled response in all situations. In this way, by defeating your tendencies, you will win the inner war—and along with you, devotion also wins.

If negative tendencies dominate certain areas of your life, you may take some wrongs steps. However, such incidents occur in your life for the purpose of testing you. Suppose a person has got angry with you. If you try to talk to him in that state, the situation is very likely going to escalate. It would be better if you walk away quietly at that time. You can sort things out when he has cooled down. Suppose you disliked the words that he used and you think about it all day long. "I am not going to let him get away with this… how dare he… I won't feel good until I have answered him back… I won't care who is in front of me, I will get even with him..." This kind of response or thinking is a tendency that stems from the ego. With consistently practiced devotion, every such tendency can be eradicated.

When an individual gives the right response to the incidents taking place in their life, their devotion deepens. Great devotees like Hanuman, Mira, Bhakt Prahlad, Tukaram, and others gave the right response to the tests in their lives with true devotion. They passed their tests with flying colors. Their lives demonstrate how one ought to be in devotion, and how devotion should become part of one's life.

Seeker: Why should testing situations occur at all?

Sirshree: We are all aware that exams are essential for the complete development of a student. The student works hard and prepares for the exams. Only after the exams, the results demonstrate whether the student has become eligible for the next grade.

In the same way, in devotion God tests the devotees so that they are challenged, and if they rise to the challenge, they will progress and move to a higher level. This is God's intention behind the tests. Because of the testing, an individual is forced to reflect upon the events occurring in their life. Incidents are a part of life, but suddenly some incident pops up which tests the individual. If their mind is shaken by that incident, they need to think over that incident and their response. "Why did this occur? What lessons can I learn from it? If this type of incident occurs again in the future, how should I prepare myself so that I can easily overcome it?" We tend to learn more from difficulties in life than we do during smooth-sailing times. Devotion places many adversities in our path in order to test and strengthen us.

People who are under the influence of blind devotion consider such incidents as karma of their previous birth, bad fortune, or God's wrath. They tend to add to their problems by consulting so-called pundits, occultists, and astrologers in a misguided effort to change their circumstances.

A sensible person learns from one's mistakes. When they inspect the mistakes they have made in their life and ponder over them, they get a profound insight. The insight is: "I should not repeat such mistakes and hence I should be tested intermittently, so that I can assess myself and prepare for the future." For that, there should be some force from nature in the form of tests. Without the force, an individual continues an endless cycle of repeating their errors in their ignorance. The external force pulls them out of that cycle.

When everything is going nice and fine, a person does not feel the need for putting in vigorous efforts for their growth. For this to happen, external force is required, which makes them put forth some intense effort that would never come in times of calm and comfort. But some people apply force against this force by resisting the lessons in adversity and continuing down the same path as before—with the same results as before.

They do not understand that, with the external force the mind is being prepared for the highest level, and the hardships are blessings in disguise. Hence, their mind applies force against this external force.

Seeker: How to be steady in devotion during testing situations?

Sirshree: *A devotee goes through testing situations gracefully by considering them as penance or sadhana. This is because a devotee has the understanding of faith and surrender.*

The mind may make your faith waver or create greed or fear, due to which you may be tempted to give up on the teachings or to disobey your master's instructions. Often people regard the Guru's instructions as bondage, as if they restrict their freedom. They don't understand that the Guru's injunctions have a profound purpose. The instructions have the power to develop your inner strength, but you miss out on that.

The grace, the beauty, in following the Guru's teachings is to develop inner strength. It saves you from so many negative things—you may or may not even be aware of what harm has been avoided in your life.

You train and control your mind when you stick to the instructions, despite your mind wavering and getting distressed. There is a big difference between doing this under force and doing it in devotion. Trying to get rid of your tendencies with force causes misery, while with devotion it happens with love for the guru's teachings and instructions. Thus, you are able to face hardships gracefully. You know what's yours will come to you, no matter what. When you remain within the triad of wisdom, devotion, and service, you don't get stuck in the illusion. Otherwise, there are so many options in this world ready to ensnare you.

So, how would your inner strength grow? How can all the

loopholes be sealed? These loopholes are responsible for the leakage of devotion. An individual always looks for loopholes to break the rules or neglect the instructions. For example, if it's written, "Please don't pluck the flowers," then someone carries off the flower pot. In this way, people look for loopholes, which in turn creates loopholes within them, from where inner strength drains away. The one who understands this topic seals all their loopholes. *What kind of inner strength did Jesus have that he could easily forgive his crucifiers! That's the power of inner strength. Devotion gives you that strength.*

Let there be enjoyment in devotion, and let there be sincerity and maturity in that enjoyment.

The level of devotion directly indicates your level of consciousness. That's why devotees are able to enjoy and be happy even during testing times.

8

100% Devotion

Seeker: When does devotion become 100%?

Sirshree: God is the ocean and the devotee is a droplet. *When the droplet merges with the ocean, it is no longer a separate entity; it becomes the ocean. That's the goal of every devotee—to become one with the beloved God. That's 100% devotion.*

But, how? It's very simple. Kittens know that they just need to meow to make their mother come to them. Then the mother takes care of everything. In the same way, after attaining supreme wisdom, the devotee knows how to call God. God comes and fulfils the desire of the devotee.

Hence, it is an essential step for every individual on the path of devotion to lovingly call out to God all the time just like a kitten and urge and pray for true devotion.

Seeker: Which qualities are required to attain 100% devotion?

Sirshree: If your aim is 100% devotion, two important qualities are required. If both are present, it's a very auspicious sign. If even one of these qualities develops, it will automatically bring about the other.

To develop 100% devotion, either 100% loving and faith-filled devotion is required, or 0% nonviolence.

Love and faith are integral to devotion, but with time people forget the true meaning of words. Hence they need to be retrieved and explained again. The devotion which has love and faith should rise to 100%. At least it should go over 50%. Your target should be 51%. So that your negative tendencies begin to dissolve.

On the other hand, your violence should reduce to 0%. This means you will have to witness and eliminate any violence occurring through you at the subtlest level. If there is violence in action, you instantly become aware of it. In the context of speech, unless we use overly abusive words, we usually don't think it's violence. We speak so many words that really hurt others, but we are not conscious of it. If we desire liberation, we'll seek forgiveness from the concerned person, if not directly, then at least in our mind. And henceforth we'll be aware of whether our words are causing any pain. Next, check if violence is occurring in your thoughts and feelings—not only towards humans but also towards objects, even stones. Stones were sculpted into Gods so that you can realize that consciousness resides even in them.

Love makes you soar high and violence pulls you down. This is the reason these two qualities are required. How beautiful it would be if both are present! But even if you hold on to one and dive deep into it, the other will start happening in your life. If you rise to the heights of devotion, you will find that violence is going towards zero. In your journey, if your love is rising above 50% and violence is dropping below 50%, then a state will arrive where both will reach their destination.

Seeker: How does divine devotion arise?

Sirshree: Divine devotion cannot arise without knowing your real self. Without this knowing, the seeker will end up taking shortcuts, finding loopholes, and basically do whatever they feel like. This topic will escape their understanding. At the most, they will call their conditional love and faith as 'devotion.' Hence the need to understand this deeply.

The individual will disappear only when true, divine devotion awakens. When the 'I' surrenders. Not just 'I' but its entire family. Each and every label that's attached with 'I'. This surrender cannot be forced. An average person will be very upset if their 'I' is taken away. Only a devotee can give up and gift their 'I.' There's a difference between taken away and gifting. One is filled with misery and the other with joy. Your understanding should increase so much that you realize that you will never get what you had expected from the "individual 'I'". Thus, when the entire family of 'I,' 'me,' 'mine' is absent, divine devotion awakens. When you get its glimpses, your heart fills up and you feel contentment. In the process, you realize that if there is no 'I,' then there is no 'you' or 'them.' There is no one except the Consciousness, except God. With this realization, you are filled with love, joy, and peace.

Seeker: What is the ultimate purpose of spirituality and its various paths? What is the parting message of this book?

Sirshree: The individual as well as the entire universe, the whole of creation is nothing but an illusion. They have a beginning and an end. They are false. The only truth is the Creator, or Self, or God, or Nothingness. Everything arises from that great nothing which has the potential of everything.

People believe that God created man. However, the truth is God did not create man, God became man! God became the creation. It is the creator and the creation. Because nothing else exists besides it. (99)

The fundamental purpose of spirituality is to understand and realize this truth. To abide in this truth, to be established in this truth, to live this truth.

The ultimate purpose of every spiritual path is surrender of the individual. Where you stop being the limited individual and become who you truly are—the limitless, formless, divine Self (which you always were). And express yourself as the Self. Express the divine qualities of the Self. (100)

The path of wisdom will help you understand and reach the truth. Devotion will help you to get stabilized in and live this truth. Thus, you attain the ultimate purpose of your life.

* * *

You can send your opinion or feedback on this book to:

Tej Gyan Foundation, P.O. Box 25, Pimpri Colony,
Pimpri, Pune 411017, Maharashtra, India.
Email: englishbooks@tejgyan.org

About Sirshree

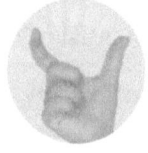

(Symbol of Acceptance)

Sirshree's spiritual quest, which began during his childhood, led him on a journey through various schools of thought and meditation practices. His overpowering desire to attain the truth made him relinquish his teaching profession. After a long period of contemplation, his spiritual quest culminated in the attainment of the ultimate truth. Since then, over the last two decades, he has dedicated his life toward elevating consciousness and making the spiritual pursuit simple and accessible to all.

Sirshree espouses, *"All paths that lead to the truth begin differently, but end in the same way – with understanding. Understanding is the whole thing. Listening to this understanding is enough to attain the truth."*

Sirshree has delivered more than 3000 discourses that simplify various aspects of life and unravel missing links in spirituality. He is the founder of Tej Gyan Foundation, a not-for-profit organization, committed to raising mass consciousness with branches in India, the United States, Europe and Asia-Pacific. Sirshree's retreats have transformed the lives of thousands and his teachings have inspired various social initiatives for raising global consciousness.

His work includes more than 100 books, some of which have been translated in more than 10 languages and published by leading publishers like Penguin and Hay House. Various luminaries and celebrities like His Holiness the Dalai Lama, publishers Mr. Reid Tracy, Ms. Tami Simon and Yoga Master Dr. B. K. S. Iyengar have released Sirshree's books and lauded his work. *The Source* book series, authored by Sirshree, has sold over 10 million copies in 5 years. His book, *The Warrior's Mirror*, published by Penguin, was featured in the Limca Book of Records for being released on the same day in 11 languages.

Tejgyan... The Road Ahead
What is Tejgyan?

Tejgyan is the wisdom of the existential truth, which is beyond duality. *Gyan* is a term commonly used for knowledge. Tejgyan is the wisdom beyond knowledge and ignorance. It is understanding that arises from direct experience of the final truth. It is what sets us free from the limitations of the mind and opens us to our highest potential.

In today's world, there are people who feel disharmony and are desperately trying to achieve balance in an unpredictable life. Tejgyan helps them in harmonizing with their true nature, the Self, thereby restoring balance in all aspects of their lives.

And then, there are those who are successful, but feel a sense of emptiness within. Tejgyan provides them fulfilment and helps them to embark on a journey towards self-realization. There are others who feel lost and are seeking the meaning of life. Tejgyan helps them to realize the true purpose of human life.

All this is possible with Tejgyan due to a very simple reason. The experience of the ultimate truth (God or Pure Consciousness) is always available. The direct experience of this truth is possible provided the right method is known. Tejgyan is that method, that understanding.

The understanding of Tejgyan makes it possible to lead a life of freedom from fear, worry, anger, and stress. It helps in attaining physical vitality, emotional strength and stability, harmony in relationships, financial freedom, and spiritual progress.

At Tej Gyan Foundation, Sirshree imparts this understanding through a System for Wisdom – a series of retreats that guides participants step by step towards realizing the true Self, being established in the experience of self-realization, and expressing its qualities. This system for wisdom has been accredited with the ISO 9001:2015 certification.

Magic of Ultimate Awakening Retreat

Magic of Ultimate Awakening is the flagship self-realization retreat offered by Tej Gyan Foundation. The retreat is conducted in Hindi and English. The teachings of the retreat are non-denominational (secular).

This residential retreat is held for 3-5 days at the foundation's MaNaN Ashram amidst the glory of the mountains and the pristine beauty of nature. The Ashram is located at the outskirts of the city of Pune in India, and is well connected by air, road and rail. The retreat is also held at other centres of Tej Gyan Foundation across the world.

You can participate in this retreat to attain ageless wisdom through a unique System for Wisdom so that you can:

1. Discover "Who am I?" through direct experience.
2. Learn to abide in pure consciousness while functioning in the world, allowing the qualities of consciousness like peace, love, joy, compassion, abundance and creativity to manifest.

3. Acquire simple tools to use in everyday life, which help quiet the chattering mind.

4. Get practical techniques to be in the present and connect to the source of all answers within (the inner guru).

5. Discover missing links in the practices of Meditation (*Dhyana*), Action (*Karma*), Wisdom (*Gyana*) and Devotion (*Bhakti*).

6. Understand the nature of your body-mind mechanism to attain freedom form its tendencies.

7. Learn practical methods to shift from mind-centered living to consciousness-centered living.

A Mini-retreat is also conducted, especially for teenagers (14-16 years of age) during summer and winter vacations.

To register for retreats, visit www.tejgyan.org, contact (+91) 9921008060, or email mail@tejgyan.com

MaNaN Ashram

Survey No. 43, Sanas Nagar, Nandoshi Gaon,

Kirkatwadi Phata, Sinhagad Road,

Pune – 411024, Maharashtra, India.

About Tej Gyan Foundation

Tej Gyan Foundation (TGF) was established with the mission of creating a highly evolved society through all-round development of every individual that transforms all the facets of their lives. It is a non-profit organization, founded on the teachings of Sirshree.

The Foundation has received the ISO certification (ISO 9001:2015) for its system of imparting wisdom. It has centers all across India as well as in other countries. The motto of Tej Gyan Foundation is "Happy Thoughts."

The Foundation is creating a highly evolved society through:

- Tejgyan Programs (Retreats, Courses, Television and Radio Programs, Podcasts)
- Tejgyan Products (Books, Audio/Video)
- Tejgyan Projects (Value education, Women empowerment, Peace initiatives)

The Foundation undertakes projects to elevate the level of consciousness among students, youth, women, senior citizens, teachers, doctors, leaders, professionals, corporate and Government organizations, police force, prisoners, etc.

Now you can register **online** for the following retreats

Maha Aasmani Param Gyan Shivir
(5 Days Residential Retreat in Hindi)

Magic of Ultimate Awakening Retreat
(3 Days Residential Retreat In English)

Mini Maha Aasmani Shivir
3 Days (Residential) Retreat for Teens

🔍 www.tejgyan.org

Books can be delivered at your doorstep by registered post or courier. You can request for the same through postal money order or pay by VPP. Please send the money order to either of the following two addresses:

WOW Publishings Pvt. Ltd.

1. Registered Office: E-4, Vaibhav Nagar, Near Tapovan Mandir, Pimpri, Pune 411017.

2. Post Box No. 36, Pimpri Colony Post Office, Pimpri, Pune – 411017

Phone No.: 9011013210 / 9623457873

You can also order your copy at the online store:
www.gethappythoughts.org

*Free Shipping plus 10% Discount on purchases above Rs. 500/-.

For further details contact:
TEJGYAN GLOBAL FOUNDATION
Registered Office: Happy Thoughts Building, Vikrant Complex, Near Tapovan Mandir, Pimpri, Pune 411017, Maharashtra, India.
Contact No: 020-27411240, 27412576
Email: mail@tejgyan.com

MaNaN Ashram: Survey No. 43, Sanas Nagar, Nandoshi gaon, Kirkatwadi Phata, Sinhagad Road, Tal. Haveli, Dist. Pune 411024, Maharashtra, India. Contact No: 992100 8060.

Hyderabad: 9885558100, **Bangalore:** 9880412588,
Delhi : 9891059875, **Nashik:** 9326967980, **Mumbai:** 9373440985

For accessing our unique 'System for Wisdom'
from self-help to self-realization, please follow us on:

	Website	www.tejgyan.org
	Video Channel	www.youtube.com/tejgyan For Q&A videos: http://goo.gl/YA81DQ
	Social networking	www.facebook.com/tejgyan
	Social networking	www.twitter.com/sirshree
	Internet Radio	http://www.tejgyan.org/internetradio.aspx

Online Shopping
www.gethappythoughts.org

Pray for World Peace along with thousands of others
at 09:09 a.m. and p.m. every day

www.ingramcontent.com/pod-product-compliance
Lightning Source LLC
LaVergne TN
LVHW041537070526
838199LV00046B/1712